D0855842

Katharine the Almost Great

The Write ~~Wrong~~ Stuff

by Lisa Mullarkey
illustrated by Phyllis Harris

magic wagon

visit us at www.abdopublishing.com

To my former students at LCS: Thanks for knocking my socks off with your stories. —LM
To Lisa Mullarkey for writing the cutest chapter books ever!! —PH

Published by Magic Wagon, a division of the ABDO Group, PO Box 398166, Minneapolis, Minnesota 55439. Copyright © 2012 by Abdo Consulting Group, Inc. International copyrights reserved in all countries. All rights reserved. No part of this book may be reproduced in any form without written permission from the publisher.

Calico Chapter Books™ is a trademark and logo of Magic Wagon.

Printed in the United States of America, North Mankato, Minnesota.
092011
012012
This book contains at least 10% recycled materials.

Text by Lisa Mullarkey
Illustrations by Phyllis Harris
Edited by Stephanie Hedlund and Rochelle Baltzer
Interior layout and design by Jaime Martens
Cover design by Jaime Martens

Library of Congress Cataloging-in-Publication Data
Mullarkey, Lisa.
 The write stuff / by Lisa Mullarkey ; illustrated by Phyllis Harris.
   p. cm. -- (Katharine the Almost Great)
 Summary: Katharine turns Mrs. Bingsley's lessons in creative writing into a competition between herself and her schoolmate Vanessa.
  ISBN 978-1-61641-828-1
 1. Creative writing (Elementary education)--Juvenile fiction. 2. Competition (Psychology)--Juvenile fiction. 3. Schools--Juvenile fiction. 4. Friendship--Juvenile fiction. [1. Creative writing--Fiction. 2. Competition (Psychology)--Fiction. 3. Schools--Fiction. 4. Friendship--Fiction.] I. Harris, Phyllis, 1962- ill. II. Title. III. Series: Mullarkey, Lisa. Katharine the almost great.
 PZ7.M91148Wr 2012
 813.6--dc23
                                    2011026393

✻ CONTENTS ✻

❀ CHAPTER 1 ❀

Boring with a Capital B

WRONG. Wrong, wrong, wrong! I glared at the bulletin board again. *Do You Have the Write Stuff?*

"No," I whispered. "I have the wrong stuff."

My essay got a C. Mrs. Bingsley scribbled a note next to it. *I liked hearing about Slip-N-Slide World, Katharine. You need to add more details. Work on your lead sentence. Try to come up with a more creative title.*

My parents call me Katharine the *Almost* Great. They say I'm a work-in-progress. I bet if I got an A on my essay and earned a Write Stuff pencil, they would finally call me Katharine the Great.

"Everything okay?" asked Crockett.

Crockett is my cousin. He knows when something's bugging me.

I showed him my big fat C. He glanced at the paper. "It's kind of short. Mrs. Bingsley likes long stories."

I gave him my grumpy eyes and said, "I know."

Crockett shrugged. "Then you get what you get and you can't get upset."

Mrs. Bingsley moved in front of the bulletin board. My stomach did a flip-flop belly drop. She said, "Vanessa, would you please join me?"

Vanessa rushed up with a goof-a-roo grin. Mrs. Bingsley gave her a paper pencil. It said *Vanessa has the write stuff!*

"Vanessa's story was well done," Mrs. Bingsley said. "Her lead sentence was super. She included lots of details." She turned toward Miss Priss-A-Poo. "Vanessa, *you* have the write stuff."

Vanessa hung the pencil on the board. Everyone clapped.

Except me. I counted pencils.

"Can you read your opening sentence, Vanessa?" Mrs. Bingsley asked.

Vanessa cleared her throat and read, "Saturday was the best day of my life."

"Ohhh," said Mrs. Bingsley. "What an attention grabber. You sucked us right into the story!" She patted Vanessa on the back. "Did it make anyone want to hear more?"

Everyone's hands flew up. Except mine.

"What happened on Saturday?" asked Johnny.

"I wanted to know, too," said Mrs. Bingsley. "A lead sentence grabs our attention. It makes us beg for more. Who wants to hear the entire story?"

Everyone's hands flew up again. Except mine.

"Let's gather on the carpet," said Mrs. Bingsley.

Tamara got to the carpet first. She plopped down on the purplicious beanbag chair. Matthew got the dusty blue one. Me? I squished in between Johnny and Crockett. It was not comfy cozy.

Vanessa climbed into the Author's Chair. Her feet dangled over the edge. She swung them back and forth and read:

A Dream Come True

by Vanessa Garfinkle

Saturday was the best day of my life. After five years, my dream finally came true!

My parents took me to Happy Tails. Happy Tails is an animal shelter. Lots of dogs live there. But they don't want to live there. They want a home of their own. They are looking for families to adopt them.

I walked up and down the rows and rows of cages. I saw all kinds of dogs. I saw a poodle, a dalmatian, three Chihuahuas, a golden retriever, beagles, black Labs, German shepherds, and even a Great Dane! Miss Lucy, the owner, let some dogs come out and play with me.

The golden retriever ran over to me and wagged its tail. She licked my face and was playful.

Mrs. Bingsley interrupted. She said, "Are Vanessa's words painting a picture in your head? That's what a good writer does."

I squeezed my eyes shut. I pictured the dog wagging its tail. Vanessa continued reading:

I played with other dogs, too. But no matter which dog I played with, the golden retriever wouldn't leave me alone.

Finally, Miss Lucy asked, "Which dog would you like to adopt?"

But it was too late! The golden retriever had already adopted me!

Everyone laughed. We laughed again when she wrote about the puppy slobbering on her shoes. When Vanessa said that Sparky had seven accidents in three days, Alex raised his hand.

"Mrs. Bingsley, I think I need to go to the bathroom . . . *now!*" he said.

When Vanessa finished, she jumped up and took a bow. "The end."

Everyone clapped. Including me. It was a good story. She deserved the pencil. Vanessa had the write stuff.

"Go back and reread your stories," said Mrs. Bingsley. "Start to revise."

I rushed back to my desk. I studied my title: *My Day at Slip-N-Slide World.*

"Vanessa," I asked, "what was your title?"

Vanessa fluff-a-puffed her hair. "*A Dream Come True.*"

"I thought your title was creative," said Mrs. Bingsley. "You could have taken the easy way out. You could have said, *The Day I Got a Dog.*"

"But that would be boring," said Vanessa.

I looked back at my title. Bor-ing!

I traced over my C. I did *not* have the write stuff.

I had the *wrong* stuff. Wrong, wrong, wrong, wrong, wrong!

And I was boring. Boring with a capital *B.*

❀ CHAPTER 2 ❀

Dollar Words

"Before everyone starts," said Mrs. Bingsley, "look at the words I underlined in your stories. I call them five cent words. They aren't exciting verbs. You need stronger action words—*dollar* words."

I scanned my paper. There were twelve underlined words.

Mrs. Bingsley walked around the room. "Dollar words spice up your story. They're more exciting than five cent words." She looked at me and continued, "Katharine, would you read one of your underlined words?"

"*Put,*" I said. "I put the towel on the shelf."

Mrs. Bingsley repeated my sentence. "I *put* the towel on the shelf. *Put* is a weak word."

"What's wrong with *put*?" I asked.

"It's boring," said Vanessa.

I stuck my tongue out at Miss Priss-A-Poo.

"Well, *put* is acceptable," said Mrs. Bingsley. "But it's a five cent word. Can anyone think of a stronger verb? One that paints a more exciting picture in our heads?"

Matthew raised his hand. "Shoved? I shoved the towel on the shelf."

I closed my eyes. Shoving a towel *was* better.

"How about plopped?" asked Vanessa.

"Another good one," said Mrs. Bingsley.

I thought about Vanessa's pencil. "I like shoved better," I said. "Way, way, way better."

Mrs. Bingsley raised her eyebrows and gave me a look. The do-not-be-rude-or-you'll-be-in-trouble look.

Oops. I gave her my most very innocent eyes. "Did you know that the pencil was invented in 1565 in England?" My calendar of 365 useless facts never lets me down. "The eraser wasn't added until 1858."

Mrs. Bingsley wasn't impressed. She sighed. "Share your next word, Katharine."

"*Walked.* I walked over to the slide."

"*Walked* is another weak verb," said Mrs. Bingsley. "Were you excited at the water park?"

I nodded.

"Then let's *feel* your excitement. Give me a dollar word."

"Raced?" I asked.

"Skedaddled," shouted Lily.

"What about bebopped or sashayed?" asked Tamara. Tamara was a dancer.

Mrs. Bingsley beamed. "All exciting choices!"

I erased walked and wrote skedaddled.

"Go through the words I underlined," said Mrs. Bingsley. "Turn those five cent words into dollar words."

"All of them?" I asked.

"All of them," she said.

By the fifth word, I was bored. Bored, bored, bored, bored, bored. I started to doodle. I pretended to sign autographs just like my idol, movie star Penelope Parks.

Vanessa slid her chair over to my desk. "Do you need help finding dollar words?" She batted her eyelashes real quick. "I'm finished. I only had two underlined words." She made a peace sign. "Just two," she repeated.

She peered over my shoulder. "You got a C?" She smiled. It was a my-paper-is-better-than-your-paper smile.

"I don't need your help," I said. "I'm fine."

She giggled a not-so-nice giggle.

That's when I spied a book under Crockett's chair. I plucked it off of the floor.

"What's that?" asked Vanessa.

"A thesaurus." I tried to remember what Crockett told me. "It gives you better words to use. Synonyms. You know, dollar words."

Vanessa scrunched her eyes and put her hands on her hips. "I don't believe you."

"Believe it," I said. "Look." I pointed to my next underlined word. I opened up the book to the L section. Just like I saw Crockett do dozens of times, I ran my finger down the page.

"Here it is," I announced. "Laugh." There were lots of words next to laugh. I read them out loud. "Chortle, chuckle, crack up, giggle, howl, roar, shriek, snort, roll with laughter."

"Wow," said Vanessa. "Those are good words." She looked at her paper and frowned.

"I could be rich with all these dollar words," I said as I hugged the book.

That's when I got an idea. If one of these words spiced up my story, what would *all* of them do?

I rewrote my first sentence. I jammed all of the synonyms into it. "When I saw how high the slide was, I chortled, chuckled, cracked up, giggled, howled, roared, shrieked, snorted, and rolled on the floor laughing."

Wow! My story was longer. Lots longer. I heart Crockett's thesaurus!

Then I felt a tap, tap, tap on my shoulder. "Are you using a thesaurus?" asked Mrs. Bingsley. "Impressive."

I pushed my paper into her hands. "Yep. I'm finding oodles of dollar words."

Mrs. Bingsley read my paper. "You certainly have added some great dollar words!"

I was going to get a pencil!

"But . . . " She bit her lip.

"But what?" I asked. "It's longer."

"True. But, you only need one stronger verb for each underlined word.

Chuckled would have been fine. Or *giggled*. But you have . . ." she counted. "Nine synonyms in a row!" She smoothed out her skirt. "That's eight too many."

She handed my paper back. "Don't add words just to make it longer. That's silly."

I found the word *silly* in the thesaurus. It said stupid, ridiculous, unwise, childish, crazy, and harebrained. I took my pencil and added three more words to the list.

Katharine

Marie

Carmichael.

❀ CHAPTER 3 ❀

Details, Details, Details

"Want ice cream for dessert?" asked Aunt Chrissy after dinner. Crockett and Aunt Chrissy live in our basement. It's been that way ever since Aunt Chrissy and Uncle Greg divorced. "We're going to the Polar Cub."

The Polar Cub had fab-u-lo-so ice cream!

I nodded my head yes. But my parents shook their heads no.

"She needs to work on her writing assignment," said Mom.

I tossed my backpack on the table next to Crockett's. "I hate writing."

Dad frowned. "Don't say *hate*, Katharine."

"Hate," said my baby brother, Jack. He clapped his hands. "Hate, hate, hate."

"Katharine!" shrieked Mom. "Be careful what you say in front of your brother. Use a different word, please."

I plucked Crockett's thesaurus out of his backpack. I found the word *hate*. "Okay, Jack," I said. "I *abhor* writing. I *detest* writing. I *can't stand* writing. I *dislike* writing. I *loathe* writing."

I put my hand on my forehead. In my best Penelope Parks voice I said, "I *am repulsed* by writing."

"Okay," said Dad. "We get it."

Jack banged on his drum. "Hate, hate, hate."

Crockett smirked. "Even though you're a bad—I mean *terrible, awful, dreadful, lousy*—role model, you have excellent dollar words. Mrs. Bingsley would be so . . ." He pretended to wipe away a tear. "Proud."

Proud schmoud, I thought. "I know I have super-duper dollar words. But I need details." I clapped my hands together three times. "Details, details, details."

Mom frowned. "You liked writing last month."

"That was before everyone got a Write Stuff pencil this month. Everyone but me. There are thirteen pencils on the bulletin board."

"We have nineteen kids in our class," said Crockett. "Not everyone got one."

"Don't get so bent out of shape," said Dad. "You'll get one soon."

Dad read my title and smiled. "Slip-N-Slide World was fun, wasn't it? Did you mention what happened when you sailed down the Claw?"

"Oops. I forgot." How could I forget? I came down the slide bottoms up! How embarrassing! My legs were above my head the entire way down.

"Did you write about the Twister?" asked Mom. "I'm never going on that slide again!"

I smiled. "Forgot again."

"What about the Flusher?" said Crockett. "You had to write about that!"

"Nope," I said.

My mom looked confused. "Then what did you write about?" She sharpened my pencil. "Adding details should do the trick."

"While you add details," said Aunt Chrissy, "we'll head out to get ice cream."

She kissed me on my cheek. "We'll bring you back a treat."

Crockett was a lucky duck.

As I glanced around the kitchen, I tap, tap, tapped my pencil. Mom's grocery list on the fridge caught my eye. Under that was Jack's diaper bag list. As I read it, it reminded me of Vanessa's story.

Vanessa's story had lists. Dog lists. Name lists. A list of everything she needed for her puppy. Mrs. Bingsley liked her lists. A lot. I tap, tap, tapped my pencil some more. Then I sat up straight and had a lightbulb moment!

I turned to the last page in my binder—my list page. I had mucho mega lists! I scanned the page. My list of all the people who voted for Crockett in the election was on top. Under it was a list of everyone I wanted to invite to my birthday party.

And didn't I have a list of every Penelope Parks DVD I owned somewhere? My pencil tap, tap, tapped faster as I remembered my list of all the flavored lip glosses I had tucked away in my dresser drawer. I was the Queen of Lists!

Vanessa may be good at writing lists but so was I! If she could get an A, I could get an A+! I started to make lists for my story. By the time I finished, I had five. Plunking them into my story was easy breezy.

When I finished, Mom reread the story. "I like your dollar words."

I smiled.

"And your neat handwriting."

I beamed.

"But . . ."

There's that but again. "But what?" I asked. Jack banged his drum. "But, but, but."

"You didn't add details. You added lists. Five long lists. I doubt that's what Mrs. Bingsley had in mind." She handed the paper back to me. "What do you think?"

"I think it's per-fect-o. Mrs. Bingsley will love my lists."

Just then, the door slammed. Crockett and Aunt Chrissy were back. They brought me an ice cream sundae.

I looked in the cup. The ice cream was melty. The chocolate sauce and whipped cream swirled and twirled together.

Crockett read my story. "Why so many lists?"

I snatched my paper back from him. "Vanessa had lists. She got an A. I want an A, too."

Crockett raised his eyebrows.

"Mrs. Bingsley will love, love, love it," I said.

But I wasn't so sure anymore. What if she thought my essay was like my cup of ice cream?

One globby, blobby, ooey, gooey mess.

❀ CHAPTER 4 ❀

Who, What, Where, When, Why, How, HELP!

Vanessa brought her writing workshop folder to lunch the next day.

"What's that for?" I asked.

"I'm taking it outside during recess," said Vanessa. "Writing workshop is so much fun."

Fun? Movie nights are fun. Dinner at Wing Li's is fun. Making chocolate chip cookies with Crockett is fun. But writing workshop? Not fun.

Lily put down her milk. "I have mine, too. We can work on our stories together."

Then Rebecca and Caroline decided to get theirs, too.

"Aren't you getting yours?" asked Miss Priss-A-Poo.

I snapped my pretzel rod in two.

This is what I wanted to say:

"Are you *nutso*?"

But this is what I really said:

"Can't. I have better things to do."

I lied. I had nothing else to do. I was the only girl outside without my folder. The boys were too busy talking about their Junior Ranger badges to play with me. So, I walked around in circles and played crunch the leaves. By myself.

After lunch, Mrs. Bingsley announced, "Class, Vanessa told me how excited everyone was during recess. So, let's continue with our stories now."

Vanessa jumped up and down and clapped. I gave her my grumpy eyes.

Mrs. Bingsley picked up a piece of chalk. "Today, I'll conference with Katharine, Rebecca, and Johnny." She wrote our names on the board. "The rest of you should continue revisions. Work on dollar words, lead sentences, and exciting titles."

Rebecca went first. Five minutes later, it was Johnny's turn to conference. Johnny finished in three minutes. He must have earned a pencil!

Then it was my turn. I slid in the seat next to Mrs. Bingsley. "I've been looking forward to seeing your revisions, Katharine." She read my story. She wriggled her nose and took off her glasses. "Your dollar words are outstanding."

I beamed.

"Your handwriting is lovely."

I glowed.

"But . . ."

There's that but again.

"But what?" I asked.

"Well," said Mrs. Bingsley, "your lists."

I crossed my fingers. This is what I wanted her to say:

"Your lists are perfect. No one can write a list like you! You've earned *two* pencils. You have the write stuff!"

But this is what she really said:

"Your story is mostly lists now." She pointed to the first one. "Although naming twenty-eight rides at Slip-N-Slide World is impressive."

I interrupted her. "Impressive enough to give me a pencil?"

She patted my back. "Not yet. You still have some revising to do. It's not about trying to fill up the paper with just any words. Why not give us some details about the rides?"

Details, schmetails. "All of them?" I asked. "That would take forever and ever!"

"No, not all of them. How about three or four? There's no need to list everything you did that day. But you do need to expand your thoughts and add details."

Mrs. Bingsley grabbed a piece of paper and a marker. In the middle of the page, she drew a circle and wrote *rides* inside. Then she made a web and labeled each part *who, what, where, when, why,* and *how.*

"Answer these questions in your story and you'll have your details," she said.

She made it sound so easy breezy.

"Well," she continued, "want to pick one and start?"

My face turned red. I took my pencil and wrote *help* in itty-bitty letters at the top of the page.

"I'm happy to help, Katharine. Let's do the first one together. What ride was your favorite?"

"The Flusher," I said. "It's like a giant toilet bowl. You shoot down a humongous tube into a wide bowl. After zip-a-zooming around the bowl a few times, you're flushed down the center hole into a pool. It's awesome."

Mrs. Bingsley looked horrified. Her eyes were open wide.

"You're not *really* flushed away," I said. "You just drop through a hole into a pool."

She wrote the Flusher under *what.* "That does sound . . . interesting, Katharine." She tapped on the word *who.* "Who went on it?"

I wrote *Me, Crockett, Aunt Chrissy, and Dad.*

"What about your mom?" asked Mrs. Bingsley. "Did she go on it?"

I shook my head. "She got to the top and had to take the bawk bawk exit."

Mrs. Bingsley looked confused. "The bawk bawk exit?"

"The chicken exit!" I laughed. "It's for fraidy cats."

She laughed. "Ah, now I understand! I've been known to take a bawk bawk exit myself. That's a terrific detail to add to your story. It's funny, too."

Under why, she wrote: Mom didn't go on. Too afraid.

Then I added the words bawk bawk and drew a chicken.

Mrs. Bingsley pursed her lips. "Hmmm. What can you put under *how*?"

I scratched my head. "I know! How the Flusher works."

"Now you're thinking! Good for you," said Mrs. Bingsley. "Answer these questions for four—"

I held up three fingers and gave her my pouty puppy eyes.

"Alright. Answer these questions for three rides and your story will be much more interesting." Mrs. Bingsley hugged me. "You're a good storyteller, Katharine. Let it shine through in your writing."

I gave Mrs. Bingsley a big hug-a-roonie. "Oh, I can shine!"

As I erased my lists, I thought of Penelope Parks. She said you needed to be glittery and sparkly to shine. Shimmery. Dazzly. I took out my Luscious Lemon Lip Gloss and slathered it on my lips.

What I needed was some of Penelope's stardust.

I blew the eraser crumbs off of my paper and sighed. 'Cause all I had was eraser dust.

CHAPTER 5

Tricky Sticks

On Wednesday, Mrs. Bingsley announced, "Good news, class! The first graders are joining our third grade class for Author's Tea on Friday. You'll be paired up with a buddy to share stories."

Everyone cheered.

"Crockett, you'll be with Emily," said Mrs. Bingsley. "Diego, you're paired with Lea."

I crossed my fingers. I wanted Beth Ann as a buddy. Beth Ann met Penelope Parks last summer! That makes her almost famous. If I work with her, then I'll be *almost* almost famous.

"Tamara, Beth Ann will be your buddy."

No fair! Tamara didn't even like Penelope Parks!

"Katharine, Dylan Thomas is your buddy."

Dylan Thomas? My mouth fell open. Dylan was a brainiac.

"I'm glad he's not my partner," said Rebecca. "He's so smart, he goes to the fourth grade for reading and writing."

"I heard he gets straight As in everything," said Julia.

"Isn't he the kid who memorized the dictionary?" asked Vanessa. She glared at me. "And the thesaurus?"

I was doomed. Doomed! Doomed by a first grader.

"To get your stories in tip-top shape," said Mrs. Bingsley, "we're having a peer editing session today." She wrote the words *Peer Editing* on the chalkboard. "Remember, the purpose is to have your peers—your classmates—check over your work. They'll help you brainstorm, improve, revise, and edit your story."

She passed out a paper with PEER EDITING written in bold letters. "Reread the rules as a reminder."

Step 1: Compliments (stay positive!)

Step 2: Suggestions (give specific ideas to make story better)

Step 3: Corrections (punctuation, grammar, spelling)

"Does everyone understand?" asked Mrs. Bingsley.

I raised my hand. "Can we pick partners?"

"Afraid not." She held up a can of Popsicle sticks. "Would you like to pull a name first?"

I stood on my tippy toes. Some sticks had small orange dots on them. I called them tricky sticks. They belonged to Rebecca, Tamara, and Julia. My favorite partners! I poked through the sticks searching for itty-bitty orange dots.

Mrs. Bingsley shook the can. "Let's make this fair and square, shall we?" She pulled the sticks out of the can and turned them upside down.

Presto change! No more orange dots.

I slowly pulled out a stick and crinkled my nose. "Vanessa Garfinkle." What kind of help could I give her? She already had an A.

Vanessa crinkled her nose, too. She turned toward Tamara. "I got an A. Katharine got a C. Having her help me is like this unsharpened pencil. Pointless."

How rude!

Mrs. Bingsley has good ears! She heard Miss Smarty Pants, too. "Vanessa! Do I need to remind you that your grade wasn't always an A?"

Vanessa's eyes got watery. Drippy. Droppy.

I moved our desks together. "What did you get the first time?" I asked as I smiled and tried to get a peek at her grade.

Mrs. Bingsley stood over Vanessa. Vanessa held her paper out. A big fat A- was on the front. Then she turned it over. There it was—a C.

"You brought your grade up from a C to an A- in a week," said Mrs. Bingsley. "But, there's still room for improvement. I'm confident Katharine will help you."

I sat up a bit taller. This is what I wanted to say:

"I'm confident, too, Miss Priss-A-Poo!"

But this is what I really said:

"I'll try my best!"

Vanessa reread her story out loud. She tossed her hair from side to side. "How can anyone possibly make this story better?"

I chewed on my pencil as I stared at step one. Compliments. "I liked your lists. You included lots of details about them."

I looked at step two. Suggestions. Then I looked at my own paper.

"Vanessa, have you made your who, what, where, when, why, and how web?" I made the same web Mrs. Bingsley had shown me on the back of Vanessa's paper. Then I pointed to how.

"Maybe you can tell us how you came up with the name Sparky." I leaned in closer. "Inquiring minds want to know."

I didn't feel like a dull pencil point anymore. I sounded a lot like Mrs. B.

Vanessa laughed. "It's the name of Penelope Parks's dog! She just got it. At least that what *Teen Times* said." Then she scratched her head. "I don't know why I didn't think of that."

"That's why you have me as your peer editor. To help!" I pointed to why. "Why did you have to wait until third grade to get a dog?"

"Do you think kids want to know that?"

"I do," I said. "I'm curious."

So she added that detail, too. Then I helped her with corrections. She didn't know the i before e except after c rule. That one gave her lots and lots of eraser dust!

"Catching mistakes when proofreading is like magic," I said. "With one erase, *poof.* The mistake is gone. We should call it Poof Reading."

Vanessa laughed. Then she read my story. I got three compliments, five suggestions, and two corrections to work on.

Forty-five minutes later, my story was per-fect-o!

"Katharine, can I see you?" asked Mrs. Bingsley.

I rush-a-rooed right up to her desk. "Am I getting a pencil now?"

"I haven't read your story yet." She handed me a sealed envelope. "Here's a note for your mother. I meant to give it to her before she left for the day. Can you give it to her?"

"You betcha, Mrs. Bingsley. You can count on me."

When I got back to my desk, Vanessa looked at the letter. "Whenever

I get a letter from Mrs. Bingsley, it means trouble."

"I'm not in trouble," I said. "I didn't do anything."

Vanessa sucked in her breath. "Ohhh, maybe that's it. You didn't do your math homework last night. Or the night before."

"Or maybe, she saw you stick your tongue out at Vanessa," said Elizabeth.

Drew poked his head over his folder. "Maybe she's telling your mom that you're still trading sandwiches with kids in the cafeteria."

I was doomed! Again.

I didn't want to go home.

Where's the bawk bawk exit when you need it?

❀ CHAPTER 6 ❀

The Switch-a-Roo

"Don't do it," warned Crockett as he sat on my bed. "It's not right."

I held the letter under my lamp. "But what if I'm in trouble?"

"What if you're not?" said Crockett. "But you're going to be if your mom finds out you read the letter." He snatched the envelope out of my hand.

"Didn't you say you wanted to be a responsible citizen so you can run for class president next year? Think of the election, Katharine! Mrs. Ammer said only honest and trustworthy kids could run."

I looked at my calendar. "That's over 300 days away." I swiped the letter back. "I can be a fair and square kind of kid later." I tore the envelope open. "One itty-bitty look isn't going to hurt."

Crockett rolled his eyes. "I'm outta here." In a flash, he was gone.

I pulled the letter out of the envelope.

Hi Carol ~

My class is going to have an author's tea tomorrow. I would like the cafeteria to have drinks and cookies available for the first and third graders to celebrate. I'll need tablecloths for three tables. You can put them on my desk whenever you have time.

Can we borrow the potted plant from your office? I appreciate your help. Thanks!

Sincerely,

Beth Bingsley

It was about the Author's Tea! Not me! Yippee!

I reread the letter and yawned. It wasn't the most exciting letter. Where were Mrs. Bingsley's dollar words? Her details? Didn't she want to paint a picture in my mom's head?

I read it a third time. The letter was boring. Boring with a capital *B*. I knew what Mrs. Bingsley needed. She needed a peer editor. Someone to spice up her letter. And I knew the perfect person to do it.

Me!

I ran down to the kitchen and jumped in front of the sink three times.

That's my signal for Crockett to come upstairs. I do not go into the basement. Ever. There are lots of creepy crawlies down there. Crockett is like a zookeeper.

"What do you want?" he shouted from the bottom of the stairs.

I opened the basement door. "Can I borrow your thesaurus?"

"Want it? Come down and get it!" He laughed as he pointed to his shoulder. His tarantula was sitting on it.

I shuddered. It was not a chuckle moment. "Please, Crockett?"

"Let her borrow it," said Aunt Chrissy. She tossed it up the stairs.

I ran back to my room and found my red marker. First, I searched for all of the five cent words.

Thanks to Crockett's thesaurus, I turned them into dollar words. Then I added some descriptive words and details. Details, details, details.

Hi Carol ~

My ^(smart, intelligent) *class is* ~~going to have~~ ^(hosting) *an author's*

tea tomorrow. I would like the ~~cafeteria~~ ^(refectory) *to*

have ~~drinks~~ ^(lemonade) *and* ^(spiced oatmeal drop) *cookies available for the*
^

first and third graders to celebrate. I'll need

^(sparkly) *tablecloths for three tables. You can* ~~put~~ ^(shove)
^

them on my ~~desk~~ ^(small writing table) *whenever you have time.*

Can we ~~borrow~~ ^(scrounge) *the potted plant from your*

^(administrative) *office? I* ~~appreciate~~ ^(value) *your* ~~help~~ ^(assistance)*. Thanks!*
^

> ^(Genuinely, honestly, and truthfully,)
> ~~Sincerely,~~

Beth Bingsley

Crockett poked his head in the door and asked, "What are you doing, Katharine?"

"I'm helping Mrs. Bingsley with her letter. Spicing it up."

Crockett covered his face with his hands. "What do you mean?"

I showed him the changes I made.

He gasped. "Katharine! You can't change someone else's letter. Mrs. Bingsley is going to be mad! Your mom is going to be mad, too." He paced back and forth. "I can hear her thunder and lightning words now!"

"But her letter was so boring, Crockett. I don't want my mom to think Mrs. Bingsley is a boring teacher. Do you?" I put the cap back on the marker. "Besides, they'll never know."

He read the letter. "Trust me. They'll know." He plopped on my bed. "I think you did something illegal. Isn't it against the law to read someone else's mail?"

I twisted a strand of hair around my finger. "I'm only practicing my peer editing skills. I'm not committing a crime. That's silly. I spiced up her letter. That's all. It was a C but now it's an A." I kissed the letter. "Maybe even an A+."

"Isn't your mom going to recognize your handwriting?"

"No, silly goose. I'm going to type it and print it out from the computer."

And that's what I did.

And just in case it was against the law, I made sure to wipe away my fingerprints.

More Major Mama Drama

The next day started out per-fect-o. Mom made blueberry pancakes for breakfast. Yum! When we got to school, she let me make the yogurt cups for dessert. I even added granola crunchies! Working in the cafeteria is one of my most favorite things to do.

As soon as class started, Mrs. Bingsley let us draw pictures for our stories. I made sure my pictures had lots of details. I was ready for Dylan Thomas. The brainiac was going to love, love, love my story. I even sketched him in one of the pictures.

After we illustrated our stories, we had free reading time. Guess who got to read in the purplicious beanbag chair. Me!

Then we got back our math tests. Guess who got a B+. Me!

Mrs. Bingsley gave me a smelly sticker for finding a library book. "You're such a help, Katharine."

If she only knew!

But that was before lunch.

Lunch was a disaster. D-I-S-A-S-T-E-R.

I spied Mrs. Bingsley and my mom talking in the corner. Mrs. Bingsley turned and scanned the crowd. When she saw me, she pointed me out to Mom.

I waved. They did not wave back.

Mom put her hands on her waist. She rolled her eyes.

When Mom rolls her eyes, it means bad news. Usually bad news for me.

They marched over.

"Katharine," Mom said in her thundery voice, "may we see you?"

Johnny, Crockett, Rebecca, and Vanessa stopped chewing. They stared at me. Everyone's eyebrows were raised. Raised eyebrows are trouble.

Diego nudged me. I ignored his nudge. I took a bite of my tuna sandwich and smiled.

No one smiled back.

"Katharine?" Mrs. Bingsley said. "Your mom asked that you come with us."

My face burned. "Did anyone know that the sandwich is named after John Montague, Fourth Earl of Sandwich? He was born in England."

Everyone kept staring.

"So on November 3, some people eat a sandwich in honor of him."

Still staring. No one seemed impressed with my knowledge. Not one itty-bitty bit.

"I'm glad you're in the mood to talk, Katharine," said Mom. "Get up. *Now!*" She lifted my tray and led me into her office.

When I sat down, Mrs. Bingsley held out the printed note. "Did you write this?"

I gave them my most very innocent look. "Who me?"

"Knock it off, Katharine," said Mom. "This is a very serious matter."

Her voice was thundery.

I slumped my shoulders. "How did you figure it out?"

"It wasn't too hard. Mrs. Bingsley has written me dozens of notes. The words didn't sound like hers. It looked as if someone went crazy with a thesaurus."

I raised my hand. "That was me."

"No one else knew about my recipe for spiced oatmeal drops, either. It was a dead giveaway."

Oops.

"I'm disappointed in you, Katharine," said Mrs. Bingsley. "I trusted you to give a note to your mom. I'm embarrassed that you felt you had to change my words. Were you trying to embarrass me?"

I jumped out of my chair. "Never! That's not it, I was just . . . " But my voice started to crack. I couldn't finish.

"Just what?" demanded Mom.

I took a deep breath. "I'm sorry, Mrs. Bingsley. I was just practicing everything you taught me. I wanted to give you dollar words. I wasn't trying to upset anyone. Honest."

Mrs. Bingsley sighed.

"I wanted to practice being a peer editor. Once I started, I couldn't stop. I wanted your words to paint a great picture in my mom's head."

I picked up the note from the desk. "Look. You didn't tell my mom what kind of cookies you wanted. So, I added details. Doesn't it make you hungry?"

Mom was mad. Madder than mad. "It was rude, Katharine. Opening private mail is unacceptable. Have I ever read your notes to Penelope Parks?"

"No," I whispered.

Everyone was quiet for a minute. Mrs. Bingsley spoke first. "I do accept your apology. However, you owe your mother an apology as well."

Mom held up her hand. "As your mother, I forgive you. We all make mistakes. But as a school employee? I'm very disappointed and angry. I feel I have no other option."

She reached inside her desk and pulled out a pad of paper. She scribbled something on it, folded it in half, and handed it to me. "I trust you won't look at it or change my words around?"

"Never!" I said. "Cross my heart." I looked at the note. "Who's it for?"

Mom pointed to the door. "Bring it to Mrs. Ammer."

Ammer the Hammer! My own mother was sending me to the principal.

As I walked down the hallway, I remembered my first major mama drama moment at school. Mom had just started working in the cafeteria. That would have been okay *if* she didn't call me Sweetie Pie every two seconds. And *if* she didn't blow me kisses when she dropped snacks off. And *if* she didn't plaster pictures of me and Bertie the Clown on the bulletin board . . .

My face got tingly.

And now, because of her, I had to visit my principal again. Last time I visited Mrs. Ammer, she thought I was a Stealie Girl! I only took those vampire costumes so I could save the school! And the time before that? I had a bad case of sassitude!

My stomach did a flip-flop belly drop as I stood in front of the office door. As I pushed the door open, I knew two things. Our visit would not include milk and cookies, and Ammer the Hammer was going to nail me.

Again.

PRINCIPAL
AMMER

❀ CHAPTER 8 ❀

Double Trouble

When I walked into Mrs. Ammer's office, her secretary, Mrs. Tracy, hung up the phone. "Back so soon, Katharine?"

I nodded. "I have a note for Mrs. Ammer. If she's busy, I can come back."

"She's never too busy for you," said Mrs. Tracy. "Go right in."

Mrs. Ammer was working on her computer. When she heard me, she spun around in her chair. "Hello, there! What brings you here today?"

I handed her the note.

She read it and took off her glasses. "I see. Oh my. What do you have to say for yourself?"

My eyes got drippy droppy. "My writing isn't that great. I got a C on my essay. I'm one of the only kids who doesn't have a Write Stuff pencil yet. I really, really, really want one. Super bad."

"Go on," said Mrs. Ammer.

"But I'm learning to be a better writer. Mrs. Bingsley has really helped me. I got excited when I thought I could make Mrs. Bingsley's letter to my mom better. She helped me, so I wanted to help her." I made an X over my heart with my finger. "Honest! So, I changed some of her boring words into dollar words. Just like she taught me."

"It was a private letter," said Mrs. Ammer. "Did you know that?"

I nodded. "But when I got the letter, Vanessa said I was probably in trouble. So, I just took a little sneak peek. Then, when I saw it and knew I wasn't in trouble, I was happy. Until I remembered that Dylan Thomas is my buddy today. I needed to practice writing.

"I didn't mean to hurt anyone's feelings. Honest. I promise you I'll never ever do it again." I sniffled and snuffled. "I'm always making mistakes."

Mrs. Ammer held up a pencil. "Everyone makes mistakes, Katharine." She pointed to the eraser. "That's why erasers were invented."

She stood. "Did you learn from your mistakes?"

I nodded. "Yep. I learned that letters are private. And I learned a lot more things, too."

"Maybe you can list them for me?"

I shook my head. "Oh no! I can't! Mrs. Bingsley said I have too many lists. But I can tell you everything I learned."

And that's what I did.

"My, you have learned lots of lessons today." Mrs. Ammer put her glasses back on and picked up the pencil. She pretended to erase me. "Okay, Katharine, I erased all of your mistakes."

I laughed. "Is that it? I'm not in trouble?"

"I think we'll leave the punishment up to Mrs. Bingsley and your mom."

Great, I thought. *Double trouble!* I raced back to the classroom. The first graders were sitting on the carpet ready for Author's Tea. Dylan waved at me as soon as I got in the door.

"Before we begin," said Mrs. Bingsley, "I have pencils to hand out. Lily, would you come forward?"

Lily bounced up and down. She ran up to Mrs. Bingsley. "Mrs. Bingsley, I was wondering, if the number 2 pencil is so popular, then why isn't it number 1?"

Everyone laughed. Lily deserved two pencils for that funny joke.

Mrs. Bingsley smiled. "You'll be reading your story tomorrow, Lily. The class is going to love your creativity and surprise ending."

"Katharine?" she said next. "Will you come forward?"

I looked up. "Me? For what?"

"A pencil, silly!"

I skedaddled to the front of the room. "I thought I was in trouble."

She winked at me. "We'll discuss that on Monday. But . . ." She handed me my pencil. "I can't deny that you've earned this pencil. Your title is funny. Your opening sentence was wonderful!

The story has fabulous details and strong dollar words. It made me laugh. Your revisions were spot on."

I jumped up and down next to Lily. I felt shiny. Sparkly.

Mrs. Bingsley cleared her throat. "Lily and Katharine, you both have the write stuff."

Dylan must have thought so, too! After I read him my story, he told me I deserved an A+++! I felt shiny. Sparkly!

Then Dylan read his story to me. When he finished, I cheered and clapped. "You deserve an A++++," I told him.

"Don't forget to put your pencil up on the board," said Mrs. Bingsley.

I grabbed Dylan's hand and rushed to the front of the room.

"Katharine, you have the write stuff," said Dylan as I pushed the pin into my pencil. Then he clapped and cheered for me!

I stared at the bulletin board. "Wrong, Dylan. Wrong, wrong, wrong, wrong, wrong!"

I grabbed a marker and scribbled Dylan's name under mine.

"Dylan," I said, "we *both* have the write stuff!"

THE END

Mrs. Bingsley and Dylan loved Katharine's story. We hope you like it, too!

Bottom's Up!

Last week, it happened! My family finally visited Slip-N-Slide World. Slip-N-Slide World is a water park. There is a lot to do there. You can go on 28 waterslides or stay in the lazy river all day long. Since I am a splash-a-roo girl, I went on oodles of slides!

The first slide I went on was the Claw. Crockett and I trudged all the way to the top of the steps. When it was my turn, the worker gave me a push. I screamed, "Watch out below!" I slid all the way down the slide with my legs over my head. How embarrassing! When I splashed into the pool next to Crockett, he said, "You should have yelled bottom's up!"

Next, we went on the Twister. Mom and Dad sat on a floaty together. They were the first to plummet down the slide. They twisted and turned so much, my mom looked as green as a four-leaf clover when she got to the bottom. My dad went on with Aunt Chrissy three more times! Crockett and I went on it four times!

My favorite ride was the Flusher. Mom, Dad, Aunt Chrissy, Crockett, and I had to wait in line for thirty minutes. When it was finally our turn, my mom peeked over the edge. "I'm not getting flushed down that hole," she said. She was green again. My dad pointed to the bawk bawk exit. "Chickens and fraidy cats can leave by going out that door," I said. My mom clucked as she slipped out the door.

The Flusher was amazing! Imagine going down a giant toilet bowl. It sounds gross-a-rooni but it's not. It's fun. You shoot down a humongous tube into a wide bowl. After zip-a-zooming around the bowl a few times, you're flushed down the center hole into the pool below.

It was time to go home after that. As we left the park, I hugged my parents. "This was the best day EVER," I said. "I can't wait to come back to Slip-N-Slide World again!"

Have the Write Stuff

You can be a super-duper writer, too. Just remember to follow these steps:

① Brainstorm ideas for a fab-u-lo-so story. Make a list or a web of ideas.

② Start writing! This is a rough draft, or a sloppy copy. It doesn't have to be per-fect-o.

③ Revise your story. Does it make sense? Can you add dollar words? Is your lead sentence exciting? Use words that paint a picture in your reader's head.

④ Edit! A peer editor can help you with tricky spelling words and pesky punctuation problems.

⑤ Publish your story! Use your best handwriting. Your final copy should sparkle and shine. Once it does, it's ready to be shared.